Copyright © 1999 by Nord–Süd Verlag AG, Gossau Zürich, Switzerland
First published in Switzerland under the title *Das Grüne Küken*
English translation copyright © 1999 by North–South Books Inc.

First published in the United States, Great Britain, Canada,
Australia, and New Zealand in 1999 by North–South Books,
an imprint of Nord–Süd Verlag AG, Gossau Zürich, Switzerland.

Distributed in the United States by North–South Books Inc., New York.

Library of Congress Cataloging-in-Publication Data is available.
A CIP catalogue record for this book is available from The British Library.

ISBN 0-7358-1071-0 (trade binding) 10 9 8 7 6 5 4 3 2 1
ISBN 0-7358-1072-9 (library binding) 10 9 8 7 6 5 4 3 2 1

Printed in Belgium

For more information about our books, and the authors and artists
who create them, visit our web site: http://www.northsouth.com

The Little Green Goose

By Adele Sansone
Illustrated by Alan Marks
Translated by J. Alison James

A MICHAEL NEUGEBAUER BOOK
NORTH-SOUTH BOOKS/NEW YORK/LONDON

In a little old barn on a little hill lived four hens, a noisy rooster, a cluster of chicks, Daisy the farm dog, and Mr. Goose.

Mr. Goose was great friends with the chicks. Like a loving uncle, he played games with them–tag or hide-and-seek. He often took them down to the pond, or gabbled a story to them.

But when the chicks were hurt or upset, they ran straight for their mother hens. And when they were proud, they boasted not to him, but to their father, the rooster. Mr. Goose longed for a chick of his own, a baby that he could raise himself. A downy little goose who would call him Daddy.

The farmyard was full of chicks chirping "Daddy! Daddy!" but it was always that old rooster who answered the call.

So one day, Mr. Goose decided to ask one of the hens for help. "Good day, Mrs. Brownhen," he said politely. "Would you be kind enough to give me one of your fine eggs? I would so much like to raise a baby chick."
"CLUCK?" Mrs. Brownhen was so startled that she almost fell out of her nest. "You're not a hen—you're a goose!" she said.
Poor Mr. Goose waddled away sadly.

That night he thought it over. There was
nothing wrong with wanting to be a father.
And if he had no wife to lay him an
egg, he had no choice but to ask the hens.
So back he went, this time to the nests
of Mrs. Whitehen, Mrs. Blackhen, and Mrs.
Speckledhen. "Would any of you be kind
enough to give me one of your eggs?
I would like to raise a baby chick myself."
"CLUCK, CLUCK, CLUCK!" The hens were so
outraged that they almost fell off their perch.
Mr. Goose waddled away sadly.
Daisy found him behind the barn, curled
up glumly in a clump of grass.

"WOOF, WOOF!" Daisy barked excitedly. "I heard you want an egg! Come quick, I found one!"

Daisy led Mr. Goose to the edge of the woods. There, on the ground, was an egg. A big egg.

"I found it! I dug it up! I dug a hole for my bone. I found this egg!" Daisy spoke in short bursts of excitement. "It looks a bit old. It smells a bit, too. But maybe you can still hatch it."

"Oh, thank you! Thank you!" said Mr. Goose.

In no time at all he'd built a nest. Carefully he tucked his huge egg into the middle, fluffed his feathers around it, and settled down. There he sat patiently, day after day, and dreamed of his little goose. He left the nest only for moments at a time, to nip a grub or sip a beakful of water.

One morning he heard a faint tapping sound. Then he felt the egg shift, and saw a crack spread across the shell.

The hole in the egg grew bigger, and a teeny little beak
appeared. Or was it a beak?
Before Mr. Goose could decide, the egg cracked open
and the chick slipped out!

It had short paws.
It had wonderful glossy green skin.
And it had a long tail, too.

"Mama?" peeped the chick. "Hungry, Mama!"

"He thinks I'm his mother!" cried Mr. Goose, overjoyed.
Daisy ran around in circles, barking excitedly.

"Isn't he wonderful?" asked Mr. Goose.
"He is," said the dog. "He is a wonderful
   green goose."

"Mama!" peeped the little green goose again. "Hungry, Mama!"
Mr. Goose fed his baby worms, snails, and other
delicious bits that he dug up with his beak. It was hard,
feeding two, but Mr. Goose was tireless, and the little
green goose grew and grew.
Every night, tucked in the nest, Mr. Goose would gabble
a bedtime story. And right before the little fellow fell
asleep, Mr. Goose said, "Close your eyes and sleep under
my wing, for you are my little green goose, and I love you."

Mr. Goose taught his baby how to walk and
how to feed himself. He taught him how to
speak kindly and to be polite. At last the little
green goose was ready to meet the
animals in the barnyard.
Mr. Goose was proud of his son, and was
sure the others would be amazed.
And how amazed they were! Mr. Goose
actually had hatched a chick. And what
a chick! They had never seen anything like it!

Soon the little green goose was allowed to play with the chicks
in the barnyard. But one day when Mr. Goose
was not there, the other chicks forgot their manners.
"You are not a real goose!"
"Yes I am!"
"No you aren't!"
"Yes I am! Mr. Goose is my mother."
"Not true! Look at yourself!
You have no feathers or beak,
you have no wings, and
you're all green. Mr. Goose
can't be your real mother."

The little green goose began to cry. He ran to the pond
and looked in the water. The chicks were right. He had no
white feathers, he had no yellow beak. He didn't
even have wings. He looked entirely different from
Mr. Goose. "I have to find my real mother," he thought.
On a stone on the bank sat a fat green frog.
"You have little feet and no wings!" cried the little
green goose happily. "You must be my mother!"
"CROAK!" said the frog, and leaped away.
"Maybe not," said the little green goose.

Out in the pond swam a fish with glistening green scales.
"You there!" cried the little green goose. "You are my mother!"
"SPLISH!" went the fish, and swam away.
"Maybe not," the little green goose said, disappointed.

But then he saw a lizard with little feet, glistening green
skin, and a long tail. He called to the lizard excitedly.
"You look exactly like me. You must be my real mother!"
"I am not!"
"Yes you are!"
"I am not!" said the lizard. "I've never even
seen an animal like you."
"But I am here!" cried the little green goose "I must look
like somebody! Who is my real mother?"
"It is certainly not me," said the lizard, and crawled away.

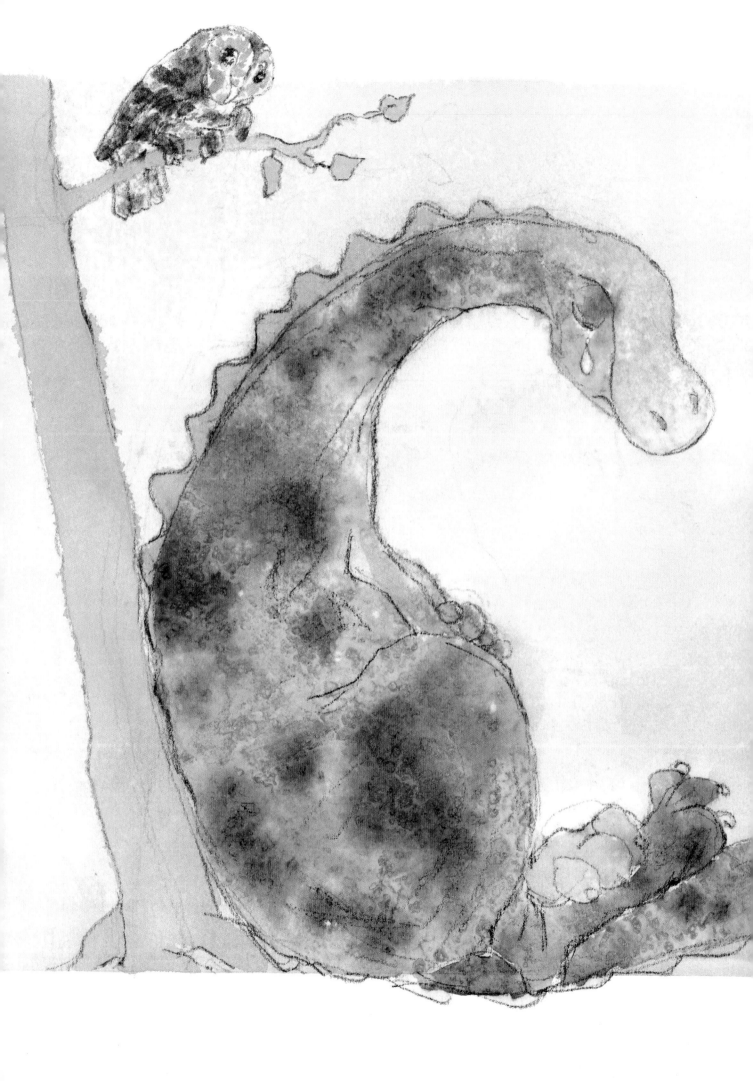

The little green goose sat down and sobbed.
"I'm just a baby! I need a mother."
He was hungry. Who would give him something
to eat? He was tired. Who would make him a
soft nest? But most of all, the little green goose
was lonely. Who would love him?
Suddenly he leaped to his feet and began to
run. He knew just where to find his real mother.
He ran faster and faster.

"Mama! Mama!" he called.

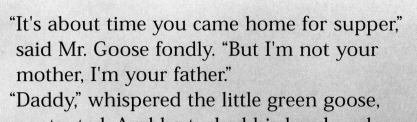

"It's about time you came home for supper,"
said Mr. Goose fondly. "But I'm not your
mother, I'm your father."
"Daddy," whispered the little green goose,
contented. And he tucked his head under
his father's warm wing and went to sleep.

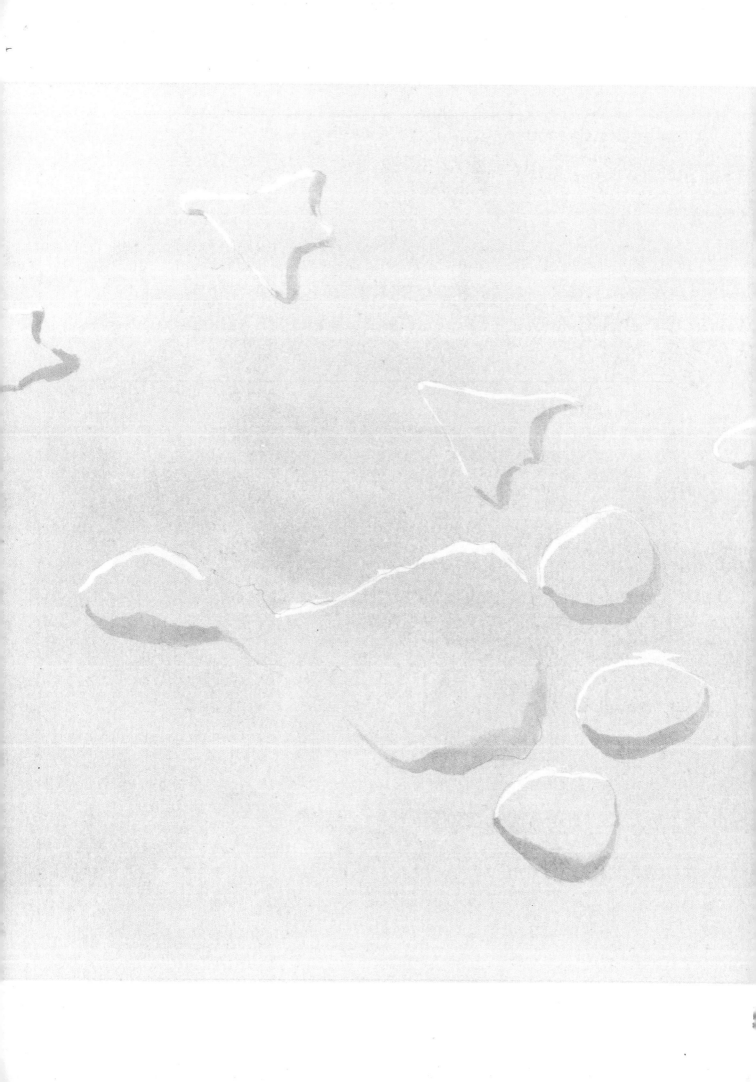